D1177538

For my family.

Starfish Bay® Children's Books
An imprint of Starfish Bay Publishing
www.starfishbaypublishing.com

THE SNOW FOX

© Rosemary Shojaie, 2020
ISBN 978-1-76036-099-3
First Published 2020
Printed in China

This book is copyright. Apart from any fair dealing for the purpose
of private study, research, criticism or review, as permitted under
the Copyright Act, no part of this publication may be reproduced or
transmitted in any form or by any means without the prior written
permission of the publisher.

Sincere thanks to Elyse Williams from Starfish Bay Children's Books for
her creative efforts in preparing this edition for publication.

hojaie, Rosemary,
he snow fox /
020]
3305249057393
03/29/21

The Snow Fox

Words and images by
Rosemary Shojaie

Nico lived deep in
the foggy forest.

On cool spring mornings, he and his friends would run to the water's edge to fish with Ava the otter.

On long, lazy afternoons, Olive the raccoon would tell them stories about the clouds floating in the summer sky.

And when the leaves fell,
they would wander silently
through the autumn trees,
because that's what Linus
the badger loved best.

But one morning, when the frosty air pinched his nose...

Nico couldn't
believe
his eyes!

No matter what he did...

...or how hard he tried...

And Nico found himself
all alone.

Was no one in the forest awake?

He looked in
high places...

...and in low...

but the woods were silent and
still, with no friend in sight.

"That's ok," thought Nico.
He had an idea.

"Ta-da! Perfect." He beamed.

Nico stared at the snow fox for
a long time.

"There's still something missing,"
he said aloud.

"How about a friend?" said a voice.

Nico gasped. A real snow fox!

"Yes!" cried Nico.
So together they rolled the
snow into a great ball...

...and found
some pretty berries...

...and made a friend.